NOW YOU CAN READ....
The Gingerbread Man

STORY ADAPTED BY LUCY KINCAID

ILLUSTRATED BY ERIC ROWE

BRIMAX BOOKS • CAMBRIDGE • ENGLAND

Once upon a time there was a
little old man and a little old
woman who lived on a farm.
The little old woman liked
cooking and one day, when the
little old man was asleep in his
rocking chair, she had an idea.

"I will make a little ginger-bread man," she said. She set to work at once. She mixed him with milk and flavoured him with ginger. She gave him a head and arms and legs. She gave him two currant eyes and a candy-peel mouth and then she put him into the oven.

When it was time to take the gingerbread man out of the oven she woke the old man. "Come and see what I have cooked," she called, as she opened the oven door.

Before she could lift the baking tray from the shelf the gingerbread man had jumped out of the oven by himself.

The old woman screamed and the old man stared in astonishment as the little gingerbread man ran towards the door.

"Stop! Stop!" cried the little old man and the little old woman as they ran after the gingerbread man.

"Run, run as fast as you can.
You will never catch me. I am
the gingerbread man," laughed the
gingerbread man. He could run much
faster than the old woman and the
old man, who could not run very
fast at all, and he soon left
them far behind.

On his way across a grassy field
he met a cow.

"Stop! Stop!" mooed the cow. "You
look good enough to eat to me."
The gingerbread man laughed. "I
have run away from a little old
man and a little old woman and
I will run away from you too,"
he said. And he did.

He ran through a
tiny gap in the
hedge, and though
the cow tried,
she could not
follow him.

As he ran through a farmyard he was chased by a dog.

"Stop! Stop!" barked the dog.

"You look good enough to eat to me."

The gingerbread man laughed. "I have run away from a little old man, a little old woman, and a cow, and I will run away from you too." And he did. He ran under the farmyard gate and when the dog tried to follow he got stuck.

In the leafy lane he met a horse.
"Stop! Stop!" neighed the horse.
"You look good enough to eat to me."
The gingerbread man laughed. "I have run away from a little old man, a little old woman, a cow and a dog, and I will run away from you too." And he did.

He dodged between
the horse's legs
to confuse him
and the horse did
not see which way
he went.

The gingerbread man was just
thinking how clever he was when
he met a fox. The fox looked
at the gingerbread man and
licked his lips hungrily, but
he said nothing.

The gingerbread man said, "You will never catch me. I have run away from a little old man, a little old woman, a dog and a cow and a horse, and I will run away from you too."

"There is no need to run away from ME," said the sly, old fox. "I do not want to catch you. Let us just walk along together."

And so they did.

Presently they came to a river. "What shall I do?" asked the gingerbread man. "I cannot swim." "That's no problem," said the fox, "I can. If you sit on my tail I will take you across to the other side."

And so the little gingerbread man did just that. When they reached the middle of the river, the fox said. "The water is getting deep. You had better move up onto my nose or you will get wet."

The gingerbread
man did not want
to get wet so he
walked along the
fox's back until
he came to his
nose.

"I can see where
we are going now,"
he laughed. "This
is fun."

But, as soon as they reached the far bank, the fox threw back his head, and as the gingerbread man fell, he caught him in his mouth and gobbled him up.

"One has to be clever to catch a gingerbread man," laughed the sly old fox.

All these appear in the pages of
the story. Can you find them?

little old man

little old woman

rocking chair

gingerbread man